Dragonterra

④

THE JUNGLE ADVENTURE

by Louise Flanagan

www.dragonterra.ie

Dragonterra Books

A paperback original
First Published in 2021

Text © Dragonterra 2021

ISBN
978 1 8383462 3 2

Set in Bembo Infant

Illustrations
© Megan Armitage 2021

Design and formatting by
Paul Martin Communications Limited

Printed in Ireland by
Spectrum Print Logistics

The paper used in this book is made from wood grown in
sustainable forests.

www.dragonterra.ie

CONTENTS

A garden kick around

Evan and Conor unbuckled their
seat belts as fast as they could when
the car stopped
in Grandad's
driveway. They
were so excited
to be spending the day here, now that
they knew all about the magical land of
Dragonterra.

Today, Mum was dropping them off.
Like Dad, she had no idea about the
secret portal at the bottom of Grandad's
garden and all the adventures they had
in Dragonterra, finding dragon eggs to
break a nasty wizard's spell!

"I really hope you boys don't cause
too much bother
for poor Grandad,"
said Mum. "He's doing us a big favour,

minding you boys while myself and Dad are at work."

The boys glanced at each other and grinned as Mum continued. "There's a football in the boot of the car. Why don't you take it with you and play in the garden? Let Grandad relax in his chair!"

"Okay!" chirped Conor, opening the boot and lifting out the football.

Grandad greeted them with a broad smile. He waved to Mum as she drove off to work, and then led the boys inside.

"It's great to see you both," said Grandad.

"You too!" they replied, hugging Grandad warmly.

"Has Lucy sent the signal for us to

return to Dragonterra yet?" asked Evan hopefully.

Grandad shook his head. "Not yet," he replied. "It might take her a bit more time to find a good place to look for another dragon egg. Wizard Snivvard has hidden them well. But don't worry, I'm sure we will hear from her very soon."

The boys nodded. So far, they had

been to Dragonterra three times. The first time, they found a fully-grown dragon named Aleeze in a secret underground cave! The second time, they went on a high seas adventure and found an egg that smelled of candy floss, hidden on a remote island. The third time, they found another of Aleeze's eggs deep in the mountains. It smelled of coconuts!

Wizard Snivvard had cast a spell to steal all five of Aleeze's eggs as soon as they were laid, because he wanted to be the ruler of Dragonterra. Without the eggs, the power of the dragons was not strong enough to defeat Snivvard. However, with all five

eggs, the dragons would be able to rule over Dragonterra once again. Snivvard had hidden the precious eggs all over Dragonterra, and it was up to the boys to return each one safely to Aleeze.

While they waited for Lucy the wozlett to send them a signal to return to Dragonterra, they went outside with the football and began kicking it back and forth. The ball soared high in the clear blue sky with every kick. Although Grandad joined in for a little while, he mostly stood and watched the boys proudly.

"Do you think we'll have to wait

much longer, Grandad?" asked Conor with a sigh. "I really can't wait to see what part of Dragonterra Lucy brings us to next!"

Grandad shrugged his shoulders. "Hopefully she will light the beacon soon," he replied. "The moment she contacts us, you're ready to go!" He pointed to the brown rucksack next to the old stone wall at the bottom of the garden. It contained all sorts of magical objects that helped the boys on their quests.

The giant nest

Now that they had time to talk, Conor decided to ask Grandad some questions about the rucksack and its precious contents. "Where did the magical objects come from anyway?" he asked.

Grandad's eyes twinkled with delight. "Well, you know that I travelled to  Dragonterra myself as a boy?" he began. Both boys nodded. They knew that Grandad had found the portal right before his tenth birthday. Grandad continued. "Well, during my first mission with Lucy the wozlett, I had to collect the magical objects. Without them, locating the dragon eggs would be impossible."

"Where did you find them?" asked Evan.

"They were in the nest of a giant bird," grinned Grandad. The boys could hardly believe their ears as Grandad continued. "You know that magpies like to gather up shiny things?"

The boys nodded again, eager to hear more. "Well, this bird liked to gather up magical glowing objects in Dragonterra!" he explained. "I had to distract the bird so that I had time to creep into its nest and take the objects! That very same rucksack was the one I used that day," he added, beaming with pride.

"How did you distract the bird?"  asked Evan in astonishment. Grandad smiled again. "My football skills came in handy," he laughed. "I found some giant seeds and kicked them like footballs as far as I could. The bird flew off after them for a tasty snack, and I had just enough time to grab the objects from the nest!"

"What a clever idea!" gasped Conor in admiration. Grandad ruffled his hair. "I'm sure both of you will come up with some clever ideas in Dragonterra, too! And perhaps your football skills will come in handy," he smiled. "Lucy might be ready for you by now. I'll go inside to check the beacon."

As Grandad headed inside, the boys continued to kick the ball back and forth and practiced all of the tricks and skills they knew.

After a few moments, Grandad came  rushing back outside, waving his hands in the air. "It's time!" he shouted excitedly. "The beacon is glowing, so Lucy must be ready and waiting for you!"

Evan and Conor raced across the garden to the old stone wall where the secret portal was hidden. Conor scooped the rucksack up off the ground and placed it onto his shoulders. "We're

ready!" they cheered.

"Good luck," said Grandad. "I really hope you find another egg!"

Whoosh!!! They zoomed through the portal, their ears buzzing loudly. Bursts of vibrant orange danced around them in the portal this time. The boys felt like they were rolling around in crisp autumn leaves. Before they knew it, they were blinking in the dazzling light of Dragonterra once more.

The ground beneath them felt quite like Grandad's garden. They stamped up and down on the soft, grassy earth. All around them, strange flowers and trees grew and the air was filled with the  sounds of buzzing insects and chirping birds. "I think we're in some sort of jungle," gasped Evan. "It's much more exotic than Donegal, that's for sure!"

They peered around them for Lucy the wozlett, eager to spend the day with her. She always guided them safely through Dragonterra and helped them to find the dragon eggs. "Lucy!" Conor

 called out nervously, his voice almost a whisper. "We're here!"

Several minutes passed by, but there was still no sign of the little creature. Eventually, Evan called out impatiently at the top of his voice.

"LUCY!"

With that, Lucy lifted the bright green leaf she had been dozing under and peeped up sleepily at the boys. "I thought I'd have time for a nap," she grinned. "You boys are usually late!"

"Not today!" they laughed. "We were in Grandad's before the beacon even started glowing!"

Lucy sprang to her feet and stretched her little arms in the air. "Let's get going then!" she said. "There's no time to waste!"

Naughty thieves

As they followed Lucy through the trees, she explained where they were. "Today, we are in the Far-reaching Jungle of Dragonterra. It's an enormous jungle, full of dense vegetation, wide rivers and deep valleys. And a lot of creatures live here too," she added.

The boys looked around in wonder. They had never seen such tall trees. They stretched up into the air like skyscrapers. All around them, huge flowers bloomed in dazzling shades of neon pink, orange and yellow, like the highlighter pens that Evan and Conor used for arts and crafts.

Lucy continued to talk. "This jungle is a likely spot for Snivvard to hide another egg. It's difficult to find your way through the jungle. Very often, explorers get lost and end up walking around in circles, trying to find the way out!"

Evan and Conor gulped. "Hopefully that won't happen to us," muttered Conor.

"Don't worry, boys," grinned Lucy. "I've done plenty of research and I know the jungle well. That's why it took me longer than usual to light the beacon

today. Let's go this way."

The boys smiled, pleased to have Lucy looking after them in Dragonterra. She was a brilliant guide and a true friend to the boys. They continued to trek through the jungle, ducking under large leaves and stepping over the twisted roots of trees. Suddenly, they heard a rustling sound in a bush right next to them. The boys froze, alarmed that it might be Wizard Snivvard! He always tried his best to scare Evan and Conor, so that they wouldn't find the dragon eggs. But to their relief, it wasn't Snivvard this time.

A furry creature sprang out of the undergrowth and sat at their feet. It looked very cute, but the boys couldn't be sure if it was dangerous or not.

Thankfully, Lucy spoke up. "Oh, that's just an elomor. They're completely harmless but they can be a little bit naughty and like playing tricks, so be careful around it!" she warned.

The boys bent down for a closer look. It had a long tail that was curled up like a spring and little hands that reminded Evan of a monkey. Conor thought its bouncy hind legs made it look more like a kangaroo.

As they examined it, the elomor reached forward and pulled both of Conor's bootlaces open in a flash. Lucy rolled her eyes. "I warned you they were pesky! It

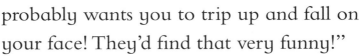

probably wants you to trip up and fall on your face! They'd find that very funny!"

"Are there more of them here?" asked Evan, glancing over both of his shoulders.

"Oh yes, where there is one elomor, there will be plenty more!" sighed Lucy. "They always live in large groups. I bet there are a least a dozen elomors spying on us at this very moment."

Conor took the rucksack off his shoulders and bent down to tie his bootlaces. Suddenly, some more elomors sprang down from the trees, snatched the rucksack, and bounced so high that they disappeared into the leafy canopy overhead. "Oh no!" cried Evan. "The magical objects! We need to get the rucksack back. We can't complete our missions without it! On the day he gave us the rucksack, Grandad warned us never to lose it!"

A perfect shot

Struggling through the dense undergrowth, they chased after the elomors who tossed the rucksack over and back between them, chattering excitedly.

"Be careful, boys, there's a ravine up ahead!" panted Lucy as she scampered along at full speed.

"What's a ravine?" puffed Conor in reply.

"It's a huge crack in the earth that stretches on for miles and miles in each direction!" she explained. With that, Conor and Evan slowed down to watch their step. Still chattering noisily above them, the elomors hurled the rucksack all around like a rag doll.

"What will they do with it?" asked Conor in dismay.

"They're just teasing us," replied Lucy. "They don't care what's inside it. Hopefully, they will get bored of it soon," she sighed.

Just then, they arrived at the edge of the ravine and the elomor with the rucksack leapt high into the air and landed safely on the other side. It sprang up a huge tree with branches that hung out over the ravine and spread high

above the boys' heads. The elomor looked down at them with a naughty grin and balanced the rucksack carefully on a branch high above them.

The other elomors chattered excitedly and nodded in approval at this trick. Then, they all bounded off through the trees and the sound of their chattering grew faint.

"Oh my," gasped Lucy, "how will we get it down?"

The boys' faces grew pale. There were no other trees near enough for little Lucy to scamper up and reach the rucksack. And the ravine was much too wide for her to jump across to climb up the tree trunk.

"Would a long stick work?" asked Conor hopefully. Lucy shook her head sadly. "It's much too high up for that," she sighed. Suddenly, Evan had an idea. "If we had something like a football, we could kick it at the rucksack and knock it out of the tree!"

"That could work!" cheered Lucy.

"Would anything inside it break during the fall though?" asked Conor.

"No!" replied Lucy. "There is nothing delicate in the bag. Magic keeps them well protected."

"What can we use as a football?" asked Evan, scratching his head. "Grandad told us that he used birdseed!" he added. Lucy smiled fondly. "Oh, I remember that adventure like it was yesterday! But unfortunately, those seeds come from a plant that doesn't grow here in the jungle."

"Maybe a different type of plant would do the trick?" suggested Conor.

"It's worth a try," urged Evan. "Let's see what we can find!" They searched the nearby trees and shrubs for something suitable. Evan spotted a jagged plant that looked quite like a cactus

but found nothing that resembled a football.

After a while, Conor spotted a plant that reminded him of a cabbage. "It's the right shape anyway," he muttered to himself. He picked it up and held it in his hands. It felt quite light and spongy, so he called the others to come and see.

"Perfect!" cried Lucy. "That will work – as long as you two can actually kick it high enough in the air," she added worriedly. The boys grinned at one another. "We've had plenty of training!" they laughed. "It was good old Grandad who encouraged us to join the local Gaelic football team!"

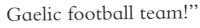

After gathering several more cabbage-like plants, they headed

back to the tree where
the rucksack was still
perched up high.

"Ready?" asked Lucy
nervously. Evan and
Conor grinned again. "For sure!" they
replied confidently. Each boy dropped
a plant down towards his foot and
kicked as hard as he could. It was much
trickier than kicking a football, but both
plants still soared high in the air, almost
reaching the rucksack on the very first
attempt!

Lucy's eyes grew wide. "I'm
impressed!" she stammered. The boys
laughed. "We were practicing in
Grandad's garden this morning!"

It only took a few more attempts
before Conor kicked the plant just right,

tipping the rucksack hard enough to knock it out of the tree. It landed right at his feet.

"Good shot!" cheered Evan. Conor felt a surge of pride and couldn't wait to tell Grandad all about it later on.

Behind the waterfall

"Thank goodness we have the rucksack back, but that wasted a lot of our time!" groaned Lucy. "When the sun sets in the jungle, it's a very creepy place to be," she shuddered.

"Let's keep going and hopefully we'll find some signs of a dragon egg soon," exclaimed Conor.

Before long, they heard the sound of rushing water. "We must be near the waterfall," said Lucy. "Let's have a look." They followed the sound of the water and soon arrived at the foot of the waterfall. As the water spilled down from above, they stood silently at the edge of the pool, admiring its beauty.

"This looks quite like Glenevin waterfall," remarked Conor. "Grandad took us to Inishowen to see it a few years

ago. He even said that waterfalls are magical, but I wasn't sure what he meant at the time," he added with a tender smile.

Just then, the air around them grew cold, and Wizard Snivvard appeared next to the waterfall, floating on his little cloud of mist. "How did you know that the dragon egg is hidden behind the waterfall?" he bellowed with rage.

Lucy grinned. "We didn't know that, but thanks for telling us!" The boys began to laugh. They weren't scared of Snivvard anymore. They knew that he couldn't hurt them and they always figured out

how to beat his nasty tricks.

"I'll cast a spell on the snapodees
to protect the egg at all costs!" cackled
Snivvard. With that, he raised his
bony, grey hands in the air. As he did so,
dozens of scaly, red creatures appeared
at the surface of the water. They looked
very like crocodiles, with large, pointy
teeth, but they also had a large fin
on their backs, rather like a shark.
Swimming back and forth, they stared at
the boys with their beady eyes.

"What can we do now?" gulped Conor. Snivvard gave a long and nasty laugh. "So near and yet so far!" he called. "And just as an extra measure, I'll make the waterfall tumble down so hard that you'll get washed away if you even try to pass underneath it!" He clapped his hands, threw his head back and laughed again. The waterfall thundered down into the pool now, splashing off the rocks all around it. "My work here is done!"

he howled. And with that, Snivvard
disappeared into thin air.

"How can we get across the pool with
all those snapping creatures?!" gasped
Evan. "Is there anything in the rucksack
to help?"

Lucy grinned. "We don't need to use

anything in
the rucksack
for this."
She pointed
upwards to
some long vines
that dangled
down from the

trees. "We can swing across!" Her eyes twinkled with delight. She really loved a good adventure!

"Even if we do make it across the pool, what about the rushing water? We'll get swept away if we dare to pass under the waterfall now," sighed Conor in dismay. Lucy's eyes twinkled again. "Well, there is something in the rucksack to help with that part," she smiled.

The boys weren't very sure about the idea of swinging on jungle vines over a pool of angry, snapping creatures. However, they tugged on some of the vines and they did seem strong enough to support their weight.

Suddenly, Conor remembered a

day out they'd spent with Grandad last summer. "Evan, do you remember when Grandad brought us to Rathmullan?" he asked. Evan's face lit up. "Yes!" he replied. "There was a rope to swing on, right beside the beach!"

Conor smiled. "At least we've practiced something like this before. We can do it!" The boys nodded confidently at one another.

"I knew your grandad would train you well for Dragonterra!" said Lucy proudly. She then explained the plan in a bit more detail. "We'll all swing at the same time and aim for the big rocks right at the foot of the waterfall. They might be slippery, so be careful!" The boys nodded again as Lucy continued. "Once we're at the foot of the waterfall, I'll hop into the rucksack and take out what we'll need to pass under it safely. Let's get going!"

Lucy perched on Conor's shoulder while Evan carried the rucksack.

"Ready?" asked Lucy.

"Ready!" shouted the boys in reply. They took a few steps back so that they could do a running jump as they swung out over the snapodees.

The creatures thrashed around in the water below the boys, and Evan had to tuck his knees up to keep out of their

reach. But thankfully, they all landed
safely on the rocks right beside the
waterfall. Now, it was time for Lucy to
select a magical object from the rucksack
to help them. The boys wondered what it
would be...

6

A powerful umbrella!

Lucy popped back out of the rucksack with a tiny umbrella in her paws, looking  very pleased indeed. The boys stared at it in disbelief. It looked like a decoration from a fruity summer drink – not anything that could help to protect them from a huge, gushing waterfall!

However, the boys knew by now that the items in Grandad's rucksack were not always as they seemed. Lucy winked at Evan and Conor as she used her tiny paws to put up the umbrella. It glowed so brightly that both boys had to look away to protect their eyes from the glare. Lucy began to tap Conor frantically on the shoulder. "Take it!" she instructed. "It's getting much too heavy for me to hold!"

Conor did as he was told and to his

amazement, the umbrella was soon the size of an ordinary umbrella – and still growing! Before long, it was even bigger than Dad's golf umbrella, and all three of them could easily fit underneath it.

Lucy beamed proudly. "In your world, don't umbrellas protect you from water?" she asked. "Your grandad always complained about the constant rain in Donegal!"

The boys nodded slowly. "I suppose so. They keep us dry from the rain at least," shrugged Conor.

"Well, this umbrella will protect us from more than a drop of rain!" grinned Lucy. With that, she urged the boys to move closer to the raging waterfall, all  tucked beneath the magic umbrella. The boys knew to trust Lucy, but they still held their breath nervously as the water began to splash down on the umbrella.

To their relief, the water did not wash them away. Sure enough, the umbrella protected them from the mighty waterfall and they were able to pass underneath it without any trouble at all!

Standing behind the waterfall, their nostrils were immediately filled with the wonderful smell of popcorn! "The dragon egg!" chorused the boys, inhaling the lovely smell. They knew by now that each dragon egg had a different smell. The first one smelled of candy floss and the second one of coconuts.

"Popcorn, indeed!" chimed in Lucy. "Delicious!" They peered around at the rocky base of the waterfall in the hope of seeing the egg, but all of the rocks were glossy and dark from the splashing water. In fact, they all looked quite like a dragon egg.

"Time to follow my nose!" cheered Lucy. She leapt down from Conor's shoulder and began scrambling all over

the rocks, sniffing them one
by one. "Aha!" she cried at
last, scraping away some
loose pebbles. "Here it is!"

The boys raced to her side and sure
enough, the wonderful scent of buttery,
salty popcorn grew even stronger. They
knew instantly that Lucy had located the
dragon egg.

"That was well disguised!" shouted
Evan, over the sound of the rushing
water. Lucy and Conor both nodded in
agreement.

"Let's get it straight
back to Aleeze!" urged
Conor. With that,
Lucy took the small
glowing stone out of
the rucksack. The three

of them knew what to do by now. They each touched the glowing stone with one hand and the dragon egg with the other. Closing their eyes, they imagined Aleeze, the mother dragon, curled up in her secret underground cave. Whoosh!!! The magic transported them there in a flash, along with the precious egg.

7

Back to the secret cave

In the darkness of the cave, they could hear Aleeze gently snoring. She was fast asleep. The two eggs they had already rescued and returned to her were tucked so far under her scaly belly that they could hardly see them.

The boys reached forward to gently touch her claw. They knew that Aleeze would hear their thoughts as long as they were touching her. Even better, they would be able to hear her, too! "We have another egg for you, Aleeze!" repeated both boys, over and over in their heads.

Sure enough, the mighty beast began to stir, her eyes blinking slowly. At the sight of a third egg, Aleeze began to jump around with joy. When she calmed down, Evan and Conor reached forward to touch her again.

"Thank you so much, boys!" she gushed. "I am so happy to have three of my precious eggs back in my nest."

The boys were bursting with pride and couldn't wait to tell Grandad. "We've already picked a name for this one, if that's ok," beamed Conor. "Elodee, to remind us of our adventures with the elomors and snapodees."

Aleeze's eyes sparkled with delight. "Perfect!" she exclaimed. "Thank you all so much." With that, she nuzzled the

egg under her belly, rolling it along the
ground with her spiky tail. Altogether, the
three eggs flickered like candles, casting
an orange glow all around. Elodee was
now safe in the nest, alongside Kipsula
and Saydee.

"Time to go home," sighed Lucy. "It
has been a long day."

"A long day but a good day!" Evan
chimed in. "Do you know where we'll go
next time, to search for the fourth egg?"

Lucy scratched her furry
little head. "I have a few ideas,"

she replied with a twinkle in her eye. The boys nodded excitedly.

"In fact, bring a warm hat, gloves and scarf with you the next time you come to Dragonterra. Our next destination might be a little bit chilly!" she grinned.

The boys smiled back at her. They knew they could rely on Lucy and couldn't wait to see what adventure lay ahead. But for now, it was time to return to Grandad's house. He would be delighted to hear all about the day's adventure, particularly about how their football skills had come in handy!

Taking one last look at the mighty dragon and her eggs, the boys touched

the glowing stone and shut their eyes.
They imagined the portal at the bottom
of the garden and… whoosh!!! They were
transported back to that very spot in a
flash.

They raced through the grass and
met Grandad at the
back door. Their happy
faces let him know
that the mission had
been successful – another egg was safely
returned to Aleeze.

"Well done, boys," cheered Grandad,
hugging them both tightly to his chest.
"Come in and tell me all about it! There's

still some time left before your dad is due to pick you up."

The three of them settled down on the sofa for a hot chocolate and the boys told Grandad all about the day's adventures. His eyes danced with joy and his heart was bursting with pride as he listened to them. Could they find all five dragon eggs to restore the power of the dragons? Was Wizard Snivvard's time in charge of Dragonterra coming to an end? Grandad really hoped so.

He was so proud that his grandsons were continuing on the quest he had started himself as a boy. And with all his heart, he hoped the time had finally come to complete the quest. Three eggs found and only two left! The boys were making excellent progress.

*Join Evan, Conor and Lucy on their
next mission, to find the fourth dragon
egg in the Snowy Plains of Dragonterra.
Check out its location on the map
on the next page. What nasty tricks
does Snivvard have in store for them?
There are many strange and wonderful
creatures to meet as they search for
another dragon egg in the magical land
of Dragonterra....*

Donegal

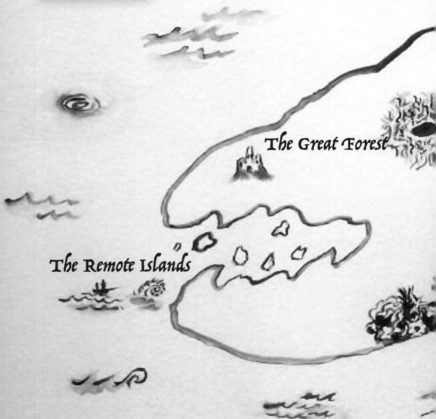

The Great Forest

The Remote Islands

The Rugged Mountains

The Far-reaching Jungle

The Snowy Plains